PUFFIN BOOKS

The Search for Treasure Island

It was winter, and Sam lay ill in bed. As the long dark night set in, he must have dozed, for when he woke suddenly the room was bathed in moonlight. And there on the floor lay his copy of *Treasure Island*.

How exciting it would be to set off for that enchanted island! The thought was no sooner struck than a voice said, 'I'll show you,' and Jim Hawkins was in the room urging Sam to follow him out of the house and away to the Spanish Main.

So began a marvellous adventure with submarines and pirates, cannons and computer banks, for Sam was not to be merely a tourist. Though he didn't realize it then, his was the vital part in a cunning scheme hatched by Squire Trelawney, Captain Smollett, Dr Livesey and the devilish Admiral Guinea — a scheme that required a boy familiar with all the paraphernalia of modern life.

The Search for Treasure Island takes Robert Louis Stevenson's classic story as its starting point and then develops audaciously into a marvellous adventure-fantasy. It will appeal not only to those who love *Treasure Island* but to anyone with a taste for swift action and extraordinary happenings.

Emma Tennant

The Search
for
Treasure Island

Illustrated by Andrew Skilleter

PUFFIN BOOKS

Puffin Books, Penguin Books Ltd, Harmondsworth, Middlesex, England
Penguin Books, 625 Madison Avenue, New York, New York 10022, U.S.A.
Penguin Books Australia Ltd, Ringwood, Victoria, Australia
Penguin Books Canada Ltd, 2801 John Street, Markham, Ontario, Canada L3R 1B4
Penguin Books (N.Z.) Ltd, 182–190 Wairau Road, Auckland 10, New Zealand

—

Published in Puffin Books 1981

—

Copyright © Emma Tennant, 1981
Illustrations copyright © Andrew Skilleter, 1981
All rights reserved

—

Made and printed in Great Britain by
Richard Clay (The Chaucer Press) Ltd,
Bungay, Suffolk
Set in Monotype Perpetua

I had been in bed for three days, with a heavy cold.

It was winter. The light outside the window was dull, as if all the colour in the world had drained away. The trees in the garden were damp and dripping, and when I sat up on the pillow I thought I could see them gliding by, like masts of ships at sea in a fog.

But in reality everything was just where it always was. The gate my father came in by was on the left, if you knelt on the bed and looked out. The vegetable patch my mother tended so carefully in spring and summer lay on the right, with a corner lopped off by the angle of the window. In winter it was empty, except for a row of cabbages and the old scarecrow, which flapped and creaked in the wind. Sometimes there was a line of washing, but it was soon pulled in again when the rain came down.

The inside of my room was as monotonous as the view from the window. I'd looked at my model aeroplanes by the mirror on the wall until I wished they would fly off and never come back. I'd played what seemed like a million games with my mother and younger sister, and I don't know which of us got the least pleasure from it.

'You needn't be so bad-tempered, you know, Sammy,' my poor mother said when she packed away the last boards of Lotto and Attack and collected the counters that rolled on the floor. 'You're getting up to-morrow, after all!'

My sister sat on the bed, thumbing through my books. This time, she was peering at an encyclopaedia and at the same time riffling through the pages of *Treasure Island*. I gave as good a kick as I could muster from under the bedclothes and the books shot to the floor. Dottie jumped up, screaming.

My mother stared at me in exasperation. 'Pack it in, Sammy,' she said. (I knew she would say that.) Then – which I wasn't expecting – 'I think we've all had enough for today. You've had your tea. Now you can sleep off your bad mood till morning!' And the door closed.

I lay in bed listening to my mother and Dottie go downstairs together. For a time I smiled in the dark, thinking what a foolish pair they made – my mother tall and tired-looking, with her hair tied up in a scarf, and Dottie short and plump, with plaits that bounced and wriggled as she walked. Then I began to feel sorry for myself. The winter night stretched ahead like eternity. And I knew if I went down to the kitchen I would get short shrift from my father. He was a doctor and he liked to come back from surgery and eat his tea in peace.

'I won't sleep at all tonight,' I said aloud, as if I could revenge myself on the streak of light that came in under the door from the landing, or the familiar model planes on the walls. 'Not one wink. That'll show you.'

I suppose I must have slept, after all. For when I

reached out for a handkerchief – my nose was so blocked I could hardly breathe – I saw the room was lit up by the moon, and the moon was so bright there were dark shadows in all the corners. The sword Uncle George had given me at Christmas stood next to its shadow by the door. The planes were as black as bats on walls the moon had whitened to day. On the floor the encyclopaedias were ranged like fallen cities, the carpet under them ridged and dappled in the rays of the moon.

At first I was delighted by the change in the weather, the heavy clouds gone and a brisk wind blowing that made the scarecrow tap every few seconds against the stick as it went round. I blew my nose and my head cleared, too. I knelt up on the bed and looked out. Perhaps the world had changed out there – or I might see my father leaving on a night call – and I could wave to him from the window and he would smile up at me. Then I could wait for him to come back, and when I heard the crunch of the car by the gate I would go back to sleep properly for the rest of the night. But I soon tired of waiting, gazing out at the garden, white in the moon. The house was quiet, except for the wind that got in by the back door and rattled the kitchen windows; and this made me feel all the more alone, as if I and the wind and the moon were all that was left in the Universe. My mother and father and Dottie must be soundly asleep. For company I tried to see pirates in the trees, waving cutlasses of black branches. Then I gave up, and settled down in bed again. It had grown cold while I was kneeling at the window, and the moon's white rays turned the room into a block of ice. How wide awake I was, and how powerless!

By the shadowy blocks of the encyclopaedias on the floor, *Treasure Island* lay open with the map of the island staring up at me. I could see the outline I knew so well: Skeleton Island, and the words 'Strong tide here', and 'Spyglass Hill' and 'Latitude and longitude struck out by J. Hawkins'. And I thought how many times, in my dreams, I'd run from the stockade to rescue the *Hispaniola*. I knew Ben Gunn so well, as he came towards me in his coat of patches. I'd fled from Long John Silver and then, fascinated, gone to seek him out again. Poor old Redruth had died in my arms. And I'd had my share of the treasure, too, buying pistols and fitting out a new ship in Bristol, getting ready to set off once more for the booty Squire Trelawney had left behind. There wasn't a reef or a tide I hadn't manoeuvred in that place.

'I'd go tonight,' I said. And when I realized I'd spoken aloud, I laughed at my own ghostly voice in the house where everyone was asleep. How could my father hear that I'd far rather be in the *Hispaniola* than at home; how could my mother and Dottie, who thought the sea was for swimming, understand the call of sound of the surf? They had little idea that I was quicker than Jim Hawkins up the rigging, and that I could lie flat in a waterlogged coracle for hours as the mutineers caroused on shore. They knew nothing of any of this, and I'd make sure they never did.

'There's only one trouble here,' I said, still speaking

aloud. I lay propped in bed, gazing at the map in the book which was scored with crosses from the moon in the trees outside. 'And it's a pretty serious one: what is the *name* of Treasure Island? It's somewhere off the coast of Spanish America, as they say in the book, but I could spend a lifetime searching in all those islands. Why were latitude and longitude struck out by Jim Hawkins? If I reach the sea, how will I steer my course under a moon that might just put me on the rocks?'

'I'll show you,' a voice said.

At first I thought I must be still talking to myself, and was drowsy without knowing it. But the voice didn't sound like mine. It was deeper and stronger, and more mischievous, too, as if its owner wanted to break into a laugh. As to where the voice came from, it certainly wasn't at the window which was behind me. Nor at the door either, still tight shut as my mother had left it.

'Treasure Island,' said the voice. 'I'm the one who knows where *that* is.'

'Can we go then?' I cried before I realized I was still speaking to thin air. And I leapt out of bed, and stood for a while, flapping my arms there in the middle of the room, and looking a pretty good fool as the mirror soon told me.

But that was the strangest part. As I ran up to the mirror, on the wall flanked by Spitfires and every kind of model aircraft, I saw that the boy in its depths wasn't me at all. What I'd taken for myself, ghostly in the moonlight and waving my arms frantically, was in reality a boy a couple of years more than me. What he waved was

a flag. On the flag, which was black on a white stick, was a skull and crossbones and these I must have mistaken for my own features. I shivered, I have to admit, in the room which seemed suddenly to have grown very cold.

'We won't be sailing under these colours, though,' the boy said as he stepped out of the glass and came up to me. 'You're Sammy. I'm Jim Hawkins. How long will it take you to get ready to go?'

As you can imagine, it didn't take me long. I pulled on jeans and a sweater, and a reefer jacket on top. The clothes felt tight, and the coat pinched under the arms, so I must have grown the past three days in bed.

But there wasn't any time to think about things like that. Jim Hawkins was already stepping silently into the corridor outside my room, and I had to run to catch up with him. As I ran, I picked Uncle George's sword from the corner, and then put it back again on the grounds that it was too babyish. It had been bad enough being treated like a six-year-old by my mother and Dottie while I was in bed with a cold. Now I was going to escape – perhaps for as long as a year – and to take a toy sword would be ridiculous.

Outside my mother and father's room a board creaked. It was so dark I could only just see Jim's shoulders. Suppose I bumped into him and we collided there in the passage, just a few feet from my father's head! I could imagine the scene that would follow. And I thought I heard my mother turn restlessly, at the sound of the board, and then settle down to sleep again.

Jim seemed to know the house well, though, because he turned right at the bottom of the stairs, and picked his way through the clutter of wellington boots as if he had always known they were there. Then he was at the garden door and turning the little key in the lock. We slipped out into the garden and ran for the trees, along the black bars of their shadows on the lawn.

There were so many things I couldn't wait to ask Jim Hawkins that I grabbed his arm as soon as we were under the first clump of silver birches. He stopped and stood frowning down at me. I saw he wasn't as fair-haired as I'd thought him but his eyes were a fierce blue. They were eyes for the crow's nest at the top of the mast, for looking out, hailing ships miles away. And his coat was blue, too, but faded – I could just make out brass buttons, with an old, different design from those stitched to the shoulders of my reefer coat.

'Jim, why didn't you want anyone to know where Treasure Island is?' I asked breathlessly. 'Is it because there's still treasure to be lifted, as you said in the record you wrote for Squire Trelawney?'

'Well, partly,' said Jim. And this time he smiled. 'But you wouldn't want the place overrun, would you?'

'Overrun?' I said, slow to grasp the point.

'The crews searching there for the cache of silver and the arms in the north-east! And the sightseers!'

'Oh of course –' I began.

But Jim put his finger to his lips. His eyes narrowed. 'Quick,' he said. 'Over the fence at the back of the wood. And on your knees for the first hundred yards!'

I dropped down on my knees, but as I ran like a cat behind Jim, I couldn't help looking back to see what had alarmed him so much. And I grinned: it was only Dottie's light in her bedroom window – and Dottie was far too scared at night to leave her room, even if (or especially if) she thought she heard voices in the garden. Jim Hawkins might have studied the lay-out of the house before coming, but he certainly didn't know my sister at all!

We reached the low fence at the back of the trees and paused for breath. I was still grinning, although I hoped it didn't show, and I was surprised to see Jim with an expression of fear still on his face. Surely he had gone through worse experiences on the *Hispaniola* than seeing a little girl's bedroom window lit up at night.

Jim shook his head when I got up close to him and put his finger to his lips again. We both stood listening, or rather, I began to realize there was something he wanted me to hear.

It was windy still and the branches of the trees groaned a bit as they met the assault. Otherwise there was nothing – no traffic on the small road that went through our village, no sign of life anywhere. The moon was as stiff and white as ever, as if it was bent on enforcing silence on the world below.

Then I heard. Tap, tap. Tap, tap. Tap. Jim turned to me, drew a deep breath. 'Pew!' he said. And he leapt over the fence. Then he was gone, into the darker trees, at such a rate I thought I would never catch him again.

'Jim!' I cried aloud, like a fool.

I ran headlong at the fence, and nearly twisted an ankle trying to clear it too quickly. I picked myself out of the damp leaves and, the next thing, ran into a tree. I must find Jim, I knew, as I zig-zagged like a shot rabbit through the yew wood. I must at once explain to him that the tapping wasn't the blind pirate Pew, as Jim had thought. It was only the scarecrow in the vegetable patch that went round in the wind, tapping the stake at every turn.

I picked up speed as I ran, and was out of the wood in little more than a couple of minutes.

There was no sign of Jim in the wide, silvery field. My heart sank. The wind had dropped in the trees behind me, and I knew that if Jim had been walking on leaves I would have heard him. Then I felt my back go cold, as if a hard hairbrush dipped in ice was being dragged along my spine.

The tapping, despite the drop in the wind, was drawing nearer. At least, it sounded louder, in the sudden quiet. And why should the scarecrow be turning, without wind?

I didn't wait to answer the question. Far away, on the other side of the field, I could see Jim. He was waving at me with the impatient gestures I had learned to recognize.

The tapping sounded in the yew trees, only a few feet away, it seemed. For every minute of that long, stubbly run over the field I held my breath and prayed. I knew old Pew was behind me, the green shade over his eyes catching the light of the moon, as he tapped with his stick on the hard furrows in the field.

CHAPTER THREE

I'll never know how I managed to run at such speed once I reached the belt of trees at the far side of the field and found Jim waiting for me. Maybe it was because of the scornful look he gave me when I reached his side and the way he leapt ahead, over ground that was snared with twigs and fallen tree-trunks. Now he didn't glance back to see if I was following either – and I knew for the first time what it was to be on your own, with the horrible, scary feeling of something chasing behind you and the person you're trying to keep up with a stranger, too. So I just ran, with branches whipping my face, and my feet aching as if they would drop off. The moon in the trees didn't help either: one minute I saw Jim's back, in his faded coat, just a few yards in front of me, and the next there was blackness. Where it was dark, it was too dark even to see my own running legs.

The trees ended suddenly. I knew this more from the lack of stinging branches against my eyes than from seeing how the land lay. And I ran on in full moonlight – until a hand came down firmly on my arm, and pulled me to a halt. 'Sammy!'

I stood, fighting to get my breath. Jim was beside me, our shadows spread out before us on flat ground and one considerably taller than the other. I stared at them, not yet daring to look up. We were on short, cropped grass; and instead of wind I could hear the sea, murmuring several hundred feet below. I pulled back and my shadow danced with me but Jim tugged at my arm again. 'It's all right, Sam,' he said. 'Look out there! Look!'

I jerked my chin up with a determined effort. Jim's voice was friendly and had lost the teasing note. It was just as it had been when he first stepped into my room.

And I couldn't hear anything that remotely resembled the tapping of the odious blind man Pew. There was only the faint swell of the sea and, from time to time, the sound of a small pebble falling off the cliff.

I don't know if you've ever had the feeling that the world is going upside-down on you. You shut your eyes and it's all black and swirling red, and when you open them again, everything is a funny colour and shape. It comes from running or spinning round too fast – or, in my case, I think it must have been the abrupt stopping of fear. The silence and the peace as I stood there were almost as frightening as the run through the woods and the bumping of my heart. And I felt a shiver of fear, again, when under my eyelids a bright gold curtain of spots began to dance.

'Come on,' Jim said. 'You've got to meet the new day sometime, Sam!'

At first, the light was too strong. And something in me said that if I opened my eyes I would enter the time Jim lived in: *his* day, not mine. But the violent dance of the gold spots in front of my eyes became too dazzling and I looked up, cautiously, half dreading what I would see.

The night had gone and a beautiful day lay over the sea and the cliffs. Sun and a blue sky, and a ship riding the waves. 'Yes,' Jim said softly as I peered, and gasped, and peered again. 'She's there. And I know the way down. But this time you hold on to the end of this. Understand?' And he tossed the end of his belt to me.

'Come on. The path's along there, to the left. If I pull sharp on the belt, stop.'

The *Hispaniola* lay before us, lit gold by the sun on the water. She was in full rig – so near, it seemed, that you could stretch out your hand to her – and at that

distance tiny, like a ship in a bottle. I wondered how far out to sea she was, and how high the cliffs where we were standing. I swallowed hard, remembering the day my father had taken me rock-climbing and had said later, more in disappointment than anger, that it would be a long time before I led an expedition to Everest.

Jim turned to me and smiled, as if he had been reading my thoughts. 'It's not as hard as it looks, Sam. And you threw off old Pew all right. You do *want* to board the *Hispaniola*, don't you?'

That settled it. I could hardly go back now, through the wood and the snapping twigs, over the field and past the vegetable garden, where the old scarecrow flapped and creaked. I couldn't bear the thought of being in my room again, with the stuffy smell of blankets and my mother staring hard at me as she wondered if I was well enough to get up. And there was the *Hispaniola*. As I looked out, I saw her shift on her moorings slightly, and swing round. I gripped hard on the end of Jim's belt, and followed him down the steep cliff to the sea.

At first, the path was scarcely visible in the chalky soil. It had been the way of sheep, perhaps, or of coast-guards, but a long time ago, for it stopped completely sometimes or ran off into crevices that dropped straight into the sea. Jim seemed to know, though, which fork to run down and which chasm to jump. He went fearlessly, as if he had gone up and down a hundred times. Even as I panted a few feet behind him and bumped up against him if he stopped suddenly, he kept his footing, held his head straight and high.

At last, when the top of the cliff was so tall behind us that it was impossible to believe we had ever been there, we stopped as even Jim was short of breath by now. He laughed, and pulled on the belt to make me sit down

20

beside him. 'You see,' he said, when the volley of stones we had dislodged fell away at our feet and there was silence, with only the rush of the sea and the cry of gulls over us, 'you see where you are now, Sam, don't you?'

The *Admiral Benbow* inn lay roughly a hundred feet beneath us. I could almost hear the old signboard swing on its rusty hinges in the light breeze that came in from the sea. An old road – a country road that had never seen a coat of tarmac – stretched away from it over low rocks. Along the road from the north a coach and horses was approaching the inn at a good speed. I watched bemused, as a cloud of white dust rose from the wheels and hung in the air before blowing out to sea. 'That'll be Dr Livesey,' Jim said, smiling. 'They're getting ready for us, Sam. We sail at dawn. Now, best foot forward!'

This time Jim let go of the belt, and I had to scramble down as best I could. Bracken and gorse clung to the lower reaches of the cliff and, by the time I came out on the slope above Black Hill Cove, my face and hands were well scratched. But I scarcely noticed when I saw how near I was to the *Admiral Benbow*. Smoke curled up out of the chimney on a roof grown over with moss. I could see blue gingham curtains in the windows. A cat sat beside a cracked pot of geraniums on a sill outside one of the bedrooms and, for a moment, I thought I saw a woman's face there, too. Could it be Mrs Hawkins, waiting for Jim to come back? What would his mother say when he told her he had brought me?

I looked back fearfully at the cliff-face, almost expecting her voice to shout from the inn that I must go back now, to my own family and home.

CHAPTER FOUR

These thoughts were interrupted by quite another kind of shout. It was a man's shout and it made me jump half out of my skin. I tried to run but my legs refused me. Only a clump of straggling blackcurrant bushes grew between the back of the *Admiral Benbow* and the slope where I was standing, quite exposed.

'Tell him I'll see to him here and now if he dares to come one step nearer,' the voice yelled from somewhere the other side of the *Admiral Benbow*. And then, 'The impudence of it. I won't hesitate to shoot, you can tell him that.'

I stayed where I was. There was no sign of Jim either. And I cursed the stupid impulse which had made me give up my bed and my comfortable home to run down a cliff I would never be able to climb up again, unaided. Then the owner of the shouting voice rounded the *Admiral Benbow* and came – or rather stumped – into view. A tall, gaunt man with a shotgun under his arm, he made for the slope at a terrific speed and then stopped and put up the gun as soon as he saw me there.

'Don't!' I yelled at him.

I must have let out a terrific shriek, because the gun went down and, at the same time, a flock of sea-gulls clattered up into the air from the rocks. And I saw, to my intense relief, that Jim was running along the road, waving the skull and crossbones. This signal

seemed to calm my attacker, for he tucked the weapon
under his arm again and came towards me more slowly,
the scowl on his face still enough to make me want
to run away fast if there had been anywhere to go. 'And
who might you be?' he said.

As was to happen so often in the course of my strange
adventures, Jim spoke out for me just in time. He
ran up the slope from the road, still waving the flag,
and he said, 'He's a friend of mine, Admiral.' Jim
turned to me, with a show of old-world manners,

'Sam, this is Admiral Guinea. Admiral Guinea, I would like you to meet Sam.'

Then a surprising thing happened. The gun went down on the ground and Admiral Guinea – whoever he might be – proceeded to make the sign of the cross before throwing himself, equally, on the ground at my feet. He gazed up at me with imploring eyes.

'Who's Admiral Guinea?' I blurted out. To tell the truth, I was hardly aware of what I was saying and even Jim's warning glance couldn't stop me now. 'I mean, you're not in *Treasure Island*,' I said. 'There's Squire Trelawney and Captain Smollett and Dr Livesey and – '

'I thought he was *him*,' Admiral Guinea was saying to Jim in low, horrified tones as I finished. 'Jim, you don't think I'd shoot a lad. Now, do you? But if it was *him*.'

'Well, it's not,' Jim said briskly. He helped the Admiral to his feet, and came up to me. 'Admiral Guinea was in this part of the country long before my father ran the *Admiral Benbow* – or before Squire Trelawney was at the Hall, for that matter,' he said. 'He lived in a house up there,' and Jim pointed along the coast road to the south, 'up above Kitt's Hole. He had a daughter, Arethusa.'

'Enough, enough,' Admiral Guinea cried, just as I was thinking the same (for what could Admiral Guinea and his daughter have to do with our voyage of discovery of Treasure Island?).

The Admiral bent to brush grass off his trousers at the knees. I saw he was quite an old man, bald on top, not nearly as formidable as he had seemed when he was running towards me with a gun. 'You can tell him, though, Jim,' he went on, in a voice considerably more muted than the one he had used earlier. 'Tell him how I can be of use, even so!'

'It's like this,' Jim said. He began to walk down the slope at my side, with Admiral Guinea following contritely at a distance. 'The Admiral has the first map of Treasure Island.'

'The first map?' I said, bewildered.

'There were two drawn,' said Jim. 'It's a strange story, really. You see, the first map, which was drawn by Robert Louis Stevenson – that's the man who invented us – well, it got lost on the way down from Scotland to the publisher. He had to do the second one from memory and it's all we had to go on when we sailed from Bristol to find the treasure. We don't *look* invented, do we?' he added with a grin.

'No, well . . . ' I stammered, for I was no longer sure if I'd been 'invented' myself. 'Admiral Guinea isn't in *Treasure Island*,' I then blurted but I had the distinct sensation that the dream was about to be broken, that I would wake up.

'That's the point,' Jim said eagerly. 'He was in a play – called *Admiral Guinea* – that Stevenson wrote after *Treasure Island* and which has the *Benbow* inn and all sorts of other things he'd used in the book. Admiral Guinea learnt about that first map – while he was still in the writer's imagination – and now you're here we can use it and go back there.' As I stared at Jim in astonishment, he cried out, 'We've got the real map and a real boy to take us there,' and leapt ahead of me, down the last slope of bracken and treacherous stones.

We reached the side of the *Admiral Benbow* and came

out on the road above the sea. Jim paused and stood smiling at the *Hispaniola*, waiting there to take us on the morning tide.

'But is there anything different on the first map?' I said. 'I mean – it *is* the same island, isn't it?'

Jim whistled as he picked a flat stone from the road's edge and sent it spinning out over the water. 'Of course it is, Sam. It's just that certain things are marked which we didn't know to look for first time out.'

I was beginning to feel confused and excited. Admiral Guinea, hobbling slightly from falling to his knees on the slope above the *Benbow*, was catching up on us fast. And, for some reason, I knew Jim wouldn't talk so freely in front of him. 'There's a form of life there, the only one of its kind in the world. It's never been discovered,' Jim said. 'And it's marked on Guinea's map, in the extreme north of the island.'

'A form of life?' I have to admit I was disappointed. And a strange thought occurred to me – that Jim and I were far apart in time. There was no such thing in the world now as an undiscovered species. It was more a question of preserving rare animals and reptiles than of hunting them down. It was enough for me that I was going to find Treasure Island, to be able to tell the world what the latitude and longitude *really* were; *that* was more exciting for me than any 'form of life'. So I said instead, 'Why did you have to wait for me before you went to Treasure Island again, Jim?'

Jim smiled. He took my arm and led me into the *Admiral Benbow*, under the painted sign. 'We need a real boy,' he said. There was no time to ask what he meant by that, or to ask who Admiral Guinea had taken me for, and why he was so fierce and so eager to help at the same time – or any of the other questions that popped in and out of my mind. For in the saloon of the *Benbow* – and lifting glasses of rum in a decorous toast as I walked in – were Squire Trelawney himself, Captain Smollett, and Dr Livesey, just disembarked from his coach and four.

I knew them at once. I couldn't count the times I've run in my dreams to the captain's cabin, along the sparred passage from the galley on the port side, and told them of the wicked plans of the mutineers. And they knew me, too. Squire Trelawney rose and came towards me, arms outstretched. Captain Smollett stepped into his path, 'I'll have no favourites on my ship,' he said. But as he spoke there was a twinkle in his eye.

CHAPTER FIVE

I was too wide-awake, that evening, to get to sleep for a long time after going upstairs.

In the old saloon, Squire Trelawney had made a space for me on the settle. After we'd eaten and drunk as much as we wanted, Admiral Guinea's map was pulled out, and we all sat poring over it. Dr Livesey made a great deal of the new 'species' we were to find on the island, and the fresh-water tanks we were taking aboard the *Hispaniola*, in case the 'species' needed water to breathe. I couldn't help noticing how Dr Livesey and Captain Smollett tapped the northern end of the map repeatedly, where a single red X marked the sanctuary of this unknown animal, and Admiral Guinea kept stretching out his hand as if to seize the map away from them.

Squire Trelawney was calm and composed, however. And I must say, the 'first map' seemed very little to make a fuss about. With the exception of a low hill next to Spyglass Hill, which was probably no more than a sandbank and worn away by the time Jim Hawkins's party got there, only the red X by the north inlet and a thicker cluster of trees than those shown on the map done from memory, indicated anything different. As before, neither latitude nor longitude were shown.

'We've an early start,' said the Squire. 'Sam, up to bed with you. How's your sea-legs, eh? We don't want any lads overboard.' And he smiled kindly at me. 'Admiral Guinea's a great man,' he went on, as if he'd guessed my thoughts. 'His bark's worse than his bite. He's had a hard life, you know. He lost his wife – and then his daughter Arethusa to a privateersman many years ago. He's a good brave man for the voyage, as you'll see.'

'Squire Trelawney,' I burst out, in this way I had of not being able to stop myself from asking questions, 'can you tell me just one thing? Please!'

'Well, what is it?' the Squire said. He beamed down at me, but he looked impatient at the same time, as if he wanted to get back to the discussion over the map.

'*When* are we? Now, I mean?'

The Squire laughed out loud at this. He called to the others to come over. 'Listen to this,' he said. 'Young Sam wants to know exactly where he may find Treasure Island. And he also wants to know *when* he is. Now, what answer can we give him there?'

Dr Livesey smiled and came over to lay an arm on my shoulder. 'Sam,' he said, 'no good came of asking too many questions. You'll ask yourself back into your own bed at home if you're not careful. You wouldn't want that, would you?'

I shuddered at the thought. Out on the sea was the *Hispaniola*, riding her moorings, waiting only for dawn to take us across the world. At home, my mother and father and Dottie would wake long after she had set sail, to go through another day just like the one before. 'No, I don't want that,' I said.

But I couldn't help noticing, on the saloon wall by the fire, the words 'Broadside Ballad' on what looked like an old poster, or parchment, and underneath, in smaller letters:

> Gold and silver hath forsaken,
> Our acquaintance cleerely:
> Twined whipcord takes the place,
> And strikes t' our shoulders neerely.

And, under that, the words:

> You Punkes and Panders everyone,
> Come follow your loving sisters.

And then what followed was obscured by a stain, where someone no doubt had thrown a mug of ale.

'Punks and panders. You could say you'll find them in any age,' said the Squire with a hearty laugh as he watched me reading. 'Now, Sam, when you hear the call in the morning, you'll come down sharp.'

'Yes sir,' I said, and I found I was saluting before I could stop myself. There was more laughter at this, and Captain Smollett said gravely that it was the captain that got the salute in the usual run, and I went up the creaking stairs of the *Admiral Benbow* with burning cheeks.

Even though it was good to find Jim at the end of the landing, signalling my room, he was as unhelpful as before when it came to answering my questions. He pointed to the bed, made a dumb-show of instant sleep, and disappeared down the passage.

I was left alone, with a hot head, and a definite feeling

that the good men in the saloon below had plans they weren't prepared to tell me. But, as you shall see, I soon witnessed the most horrible and abominable act, and heard a good deal that should have dissuaded me from embarking on the *Hispaniola* in the morning. It didn't, but I still wonder, when I think of that journey to Treasure Island, how I came back home alive.

CHAPTER SIX

I was woken from a dream by the tapping sound again. As it had taken me a good time to get off to sleep, I was still muzzy, and I lay in bed with my legs as unmoveable as trees. The dream I'd had made it worse, for I dreamed myself on an island with a crowd of giant snails, and one of them had come right down on me with its shell, crushing me under its huge, scaly lid. As I struggled to escape, my feet beat uselessly on the ground and I'll never know whether they tapped in my dream or whether this was the first time I felt the approach of Blind Pew. As he made his way along the passage of the *Admiral Benbow*, I heard the words of a song, sung in a horrible low growl of a voice, 'It's time for us to go, it's time for us to go,' – and I fought to sit up in bed.

When I finally succeeded, it was to find that Pew had tapped his way into the room next to mine. He must have been standing right up against the wall there, for every word came through as clear as if there had been nothing but thin air between us.

The first muffled shout wasn't from Pew, though, and I recognized Admiral Guinea, in the tone he'd used on me that afternoon. 'You . . . you! I knew you were coming . . . I'm ready for you, Pew. God help me, so I am.'

And there was a terrible clatter of a sword (rusty by the sound of it) being pulled from a scabbard, and a table going over and Admiral Guinea cursing. Pew must have nipped away, used to the darkness as he was, and the next thing was his voice, 'What's that? Eh?' in a whisper that came straight through the wall and made me draw back and almost fall out of the bed. Silence for a while, and I sat trembling. 'Guinea, you old rogue, I want that map. That *map*, Admiral m'lud, and look smart to it now.'

'Pew, you'll get no map from me. I know what you're looking for, Pew. Over my dead body you'll ever lay your hands on it!'

There was another crash as some small piece of furniture went down, and Admiral Guinea continued, this time in a quieter tone, but just as menacing, 'You shipped with Flint the pirate, Pew. You were the scandal of the Guinea coast from Lagos down to Calabar. We're honest men, and we've a new boy along with us this time. We'll show him the treasures Nature left on that island and none other. Now get out of here, and fast, or I wake the inn and Trelawney claps you in.'

'Now, now,' groaned Pew, 'you can't get away with that so fast, Guinea. You with the slaving ships, and the wife what died of grief at you, and the lovely Arethusa going off with that lying sailor — you speak of Nature's treasures — hah!'

Now it was Admiral Guinea's turn to groan. 'That's over and done with, Pew! Now let yourself out of here and no more of it!'

But the Admiral's voice sounded weaker, I thought. And Pew must have seen his advantage, for he added, in a particularly unpleasant, hissing tone, 'The Negro lass, Admiral, remember, as what we both wanted one fine day? And how we had it out with p'int and edge on Lagos sands? So you're a gentleman now, Admiral, but you was always keen on the doubloons, you'll agree. Show me that map, guv, and we'll go halves on the treasure there – take the word of a gentleman of fortune on that!'

This speech was followed, then, by a sound I can't try to describe. I would know it at once if I ever heard it again. And I hope I never do.

Admiral Guinea must have recovered his agility as Pew was speaking for there was a sudden lunge – Guinea must have got Pew by the throat and the horrible noise started up of breath choked out until it came to an end.

I dived under the bedclothes. And I lay there until I could hardly breathe, myself. Something told me, though, that if I shouted and summoned help, there would be no setting off in the *Hispaniola* in the morning. The authorities would be called. We'd end up marooned in the *Benbow* inn. So I kept silent, while Admiral Guinea stumbled about in the next room, tying up Pew's body or hiding it, I daresay, but I didn't like to think of that too much. I closed my eyes and tried to get to sleep again. When I did sleep, my dreams were stranger than before. And I could have sworn, whenever I half-awoke and fell off to sleep again, that I could

hear in the passage outside old Pew's voice and it went on monotonously, in that low hissing tone:

> 'Time for us to go,
> Time for us to go,
> And we'll keep the brig three p'ints away,
> For it's time for us to go!'

CHAPTER SEVEN

The next day dawned light and fresh. I had little time
to think of Blind Pew, or Admiral Guinea's strange past,
or the real meaning of the red cross on the map. I had
to run to keep up with Jim and the men as they marched
down the road to the south of the inn. And when they
went down to the cove, where a rowing-boat lay ready,
I kept silence with the rest of them, as they stowed
away bags and made general preparation.

The *Hispaniola* was as perfect a two-masted schooner
as she had been in the drawings in my copy of *Treasure
Island*. Better still, she was no longer just a black and
white picture but real wood and sail with a hull painted
deep blue. There was a swivel amidships and a long
brass nine. By the time I'd run twice round her and
seen the six berths astern, I could really believe she
existed and that I was going to sail in her at last. A
number of men came aboard while I was doing all this,
and Jim explained they were our crew, carefully picked
by Captain Smollett in Bristol. 'So no Long John Silver
this time,' I said. And again, I have to admit I was
disappointed though why anyone would want the mutineers on board after hearing Blind Pew last night, I
couldn't say.

Jim burst out laughing. 'You'll never see those men,
Sam,' he said. '*Drink and the devil looked after the rest*.
They're all safely in hell, if safely's the word for it.

But old Tom Redruth, the Squire's friend, he's one of the crew. Squire Trelawney reckoned he deserved a reward.'

I thought of poor Redruth, dying at the hands of the pirates, and nodded agreement. And, as I saw the sailors going about on deck and carrying the stores down to the hold, I felt glad to be in their company. There wasn't the slightest sign then, with the sun coming up in a blue sky, and a few wisps of cloud, and a light wind filling out the sails as we slipped away from the coast, of the troubles these honest but dull men would bring us.

All I can report of our first day in the Atlantic Ocean is that the *Hispaniola* went like a bird, even in fairly high seas, and was clearly in excellent condition.

It was odd, in this mix-up of time I was living, to see the great jets overhead, carrying passengers to and from America. And I saw Concorde once, high above us, but when I pointed it out to Jim he glanced up at the sky and gave an angry shrug. 'We can't see these things, Sam,' he said. 'It's not fair if you show off about them. I can't even *imagine* what they're like!' And he sighed.

'But how about – well, the big tankers for instance,' I said. For I worried suddenly that we might have a collision at sea, if all modern inventions were invisible to the captain and his crew. I tried to calculate just *when* they all were and I wished Squire Trelawney had answered my question in the *Benbow* inn the night before. Their clothes looked eighteenth century, as I remembered from the history books at school, although it was hard

to tell with Jim, as his coat and trousers were so tattered
and patched. But the author of *Treasure Island* had
lived a hundred years later. Were they really of his time,
which would explain their interest in this new 'form of
life' on the island? It occurred to me that I might be
sailing in the company of men in the age of Darwin –
men whose eyes were just opening to a new scientific
age.

Jim laughed again, but his expression was less friendly.
'Why d'you think you're here, Sam?' he said. I felt
afraid, as if something bad was coming my way. I
wondered if the great planes could see the *Hispaniola* –
if I would ever go back into the modern world. 'You're

for the look-out,' Jim said. 'Up there!' He pointed to the top of the mast. It made me giddy to look up at that height. 'You've heard of the crow's nest? Well, that's your home until we're safely over the sea.'

'At night too?' I cried before I could look as if running up to the crow's nest would be no trouble at all.

'No. At night they have lights and we can see them – light is the one thing from your time we *can* see. All day, though, you'll be up there. You'll get used to it, Sam.'

At that moment, as if waiting for Jim to finish, Captain Smollett paced across the deck and stood in front of me. 'Take up stations, Sam,' he said. 'Dawn at five bells. You'll keep your cabin astern. And report instantly on sighting any vessel in our path.'

'Aye, aye, sir,' I said and set off, to cling to rope that lurched at every movement of the ship and to struggle to keep my footing as Jim stood, shouting encouragement, on the deck below.

How I reached the crow's nest I'll never know – but I did, and once I was up there I felt I was really on top of the world.

The English coast was already only a haze behind us. Ahead lay the ocean, miles and miles of it. If I did wish for a moment that I was aboard a plane and covering that great stretch of water at the speed of the late-twentieth century, I soon reminded myself that only the *Hispaniola* could take me to the real Treasure Island.

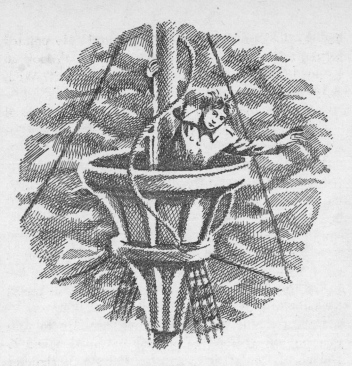

I liked the way the ship creaked gently, too, and the
sails tautened and went slack below me in the wind. It
was more real, somehow, than those monsters of the
air. From high up, I had the pleasant feeling that only I
and the *Hispaniola* were on our way to that mysterious
island off the coast of Spanish South America and that
I was steering her, effortlessly, over the sea.

There were other reasons, as well, why I got to like
the crow's nest, and looked forward in the mornings to
that horrible climb up the rigging. It was like this.

I slept astern, on the lower of two bunks, with Jim

in the bunk over my head. On the port side was Dr Livesey's cabin, on the starboard was Squire Trelawney's (Captain Smollett, of course, had the Captain's cabin) and further on from Squire Trelawney was old Redruth, who had Admiral Guinea as his neighbour.

Now what I didn't like was the way Jim and I were always left out of things in the evenings. We'd all have dinner in the Captain's cabin (brought by Redruth, the new ship's cook, and he was neither as entertaining nor as good a cook as Long John Silver must have been). As soon as the meal was over, Squire Trelawney and Admiral Guinea exchanged glances, and Captain Smollett watched them doing so, and then he turned to me or to Jim and said, 'Along with you, boy.'

And that was that. There was no choice but to leave the table and go out to stroll on deck if it was warm enough or sit in the cabin if it was cold. The kitchen was no fun to visit, as old Redruth was silent and dour. The crew, who settled in their hammocks early, had none of the rum ration the Squire had so rashly supplied on the first trip, and they didn't even sing shanties to make the long evenings pass quicker.

The other thing was that the assorted company in the Captain's cabin only appeared to notice they had one boy with them. Sometimes they talked to me directly and ignored Jim, and sometimes it was the other way about. It was a funny feeling. And as Jim, too, was very unpredictable in his behaviour towards me – friendly one day and nose-in-the-air and sulky the next – it was no wonder I waited eagerly for morning and my time alone in the crow's nest. I sometimes told myself that it was only because of the other boys at school that I was still pleased to be going to Treasure Island. I thought of their faces when I told them I'd actually been there and what its name was, as well. But on the days Jim was a friend of mine, I soon forgot all about the boys at school. The Squire and the rest were nice enough, too, when it wasn't after-supper-time in the smoke-filled Captain's cabin.

When we'd been at sea twenty days, and I'd grown so used to our life that I'd almost forgotten home, something happened which changed our course dramatically.

Supper was over in the Captain's cabin and Redruth had cleared it away, leaving Squire Trelawney and Admiral Guinea free to give the signal for Jim and me to go. The talk had been about the strange life we'd find on the island, and how we must bring the specimens back safely, with the food they would need on the journey packed in damp moss to stop it from going bad. I was just reflecting on the wonders of refrigeration, unknown to them of course, when Admiral Guinea (he had drunk more wine than usual) said, 'And if they get there first? What then, Squire?'

A silence followed this. Normally, Captain Smollett would already have ordered us from the cabin but he appeared so taken aback by Guinea's remark that he just sat there staring at him as if he couldn't believe his ears. 'I mean,' Admiral Guinea went on, 'they might've got there already. Who knows where they'd have hidden it by now.' And he pulled the map from his coat pocket. Several hands came forward to smooth it down on the table and I thought suddenly that this was what they did every evening when 'the boy' was no longer wanted there.

'We'll cover north and north-east in two parties then, and meet up at the stockade,' said Dr Livesey. He looked different, somehow, that evening, his face was flushed and his speech quick. 'If we *did* all go to the north inlet, and they were there and came up behind us – ' He broke off. 'Good heavens, Cap'n Smollett, it seems we're not alone here tonight.'

Captain Smollett swung round in his chair, saw us, and glared. 'It's time to say good-night, boy,' he said quietly. 'Haven't got into the way of it all this time, have you?'

Jim and I were out in the passage-way and the cabin door was closed behind us before there was time even to mumble an apology. We stood there, then Jim made his way up to the deck and I followed. 'Jim,' I said, as we leaned on the rail and looked down at the water, which was lit here and there by the lanterns from Redruth's kitchen and the crew's quarters. 'What's going on? What are they really looking for – it's treasure, isn't it?'

Jim sighed. He went on staring down at the furrow the *Hispaniola* made in the water, and the occasional wave, specked with foam, which came towards us like a small hill and then collapsed under us. 'I don't know,' he said. 'I really did think, when Squire Trelawney

46

told me we were ready for another voyage and that I was to go and fetch you, well, that it was for the purpose of finding these specimens of rare life. He said we needed you as our look-out, and that's true enough. But now I'm beginning to wonder – '

Then I told Jim about Pew. Jim turned to look at me at last, as I described the terrible tapping in the passage, and the fight between Admiral Guinea and Pew, and Pew's choking death. Jim whistled, reminding me suddenly of the time he'd bent to pick up a stone outside the *Benbow* inn and whistled as he sent it skimming over the sea. 'Sam,' he said quietly. 'If Pew was after Admiral Guinea's map, there *must* still be treasure there. Or a different kind of treasure, that was never marked on the map we had.'

'I thought we'd never set sail if I told anyone,' I replied, and Jim must have known I was telling the truth because he nodded, and detached an arm from the ship's rail to pat me on the shoulder.

'You were right,' he said. 'Pew's murderer would've had to be taken to trial. And,' – he whistled again at the realization of it, 'that's Admiral Guinea, of course. He wouldn't have been on board with us. And without Guinea and his map, I doubt the Squire and Cap'n Smollett would have wanted to go to Treasure Island after all.'

'So Squire Trelawney and the rest of them aren't so different from old Pew,' I said. 'I mean, they all want treasure!'

Jim was shocked by this. I could hardly understand

his old-fashioned language when he said: 'They're King's men, Sam. Old Pew was a pirate, a vagabond – and so were the rest of Captain Flint's crew. You mustn't speak like that about our Captain, Sam.'

I was about to ask what the Squire and his confederates were likely to do with the treasure when they found it – would they give it to the nation, or charity, or a museum? (surely it must be different from the old days when you just went off with it and did as you pleased) – when something floating alongside in the water made me jump up so smartly that I nearly knocked Jim over the rail. 'Quick!' I gasped, when I could get my breath. 'Run to the Captain's cabin! Tell him we must go about at once!'

'What? Why?' Jim cried.

It was then that I remembered. Jim couldn't see things from my world, except lights at night. And the thing that coiled and slithered towards us, like a giant black snake, certainly had no light in it, though it would become a raging path of fire if it oozed into the ship and caught the candles in our lanterns below. 'An oil slick,' I yelled at Jim, who looked at me as blankly as if I'd just said a word in Chinese. 'Hurry, hurry, or we're lost!'

The next ten minutes were like one of those speeded-up cartoon films where people run and fall flat on their faces, and things drop out of the sky and fall with a loud crash.

Jim ran to the Captain's cabin. Captain Smollett and the Squire and Dr Livesey and Admiral Guinea were up on deck ten seconds later, still flushed and wild-eyed from their conversation over the map. Captain Smollett shouted orders to the crew. The deck was soon swarming with hands and the *Hispaniola* shuddered as the boom swung and she went about. In all this, Captain Smollett kept his hand firmly on my shoulder and told me that I must warn him of this dangerous river of oil, which he couldn't see. He had difficulty believing me, I knew – but he had no choice – and at times his hand dug so hard into my back that I might have been under arrest for a crime. 'We'll be off course,' he muttered, as we sped away from the slick, into a night with a windy sky and clouds racing over the moon. 'How long is this damned thing, boy?'

Obviously, I couldn't answer. Once the oil lay to stern, it soon merged into the blackness of the water and, for all my 'magical' powers of being able to detect this strange phenomenon of the future, I was as blind as he was to its actual extent. 'I'll be able to tell you at daybreak, sir,' I said, when the violent movement of the *Hispaniola* had died down and the hands were hauling in the mainsail in the rising wind. 'I'll go up, sir, to the look-out.'

At this, Captain Smollett gave me one of his rare, approving looks. He knew, perhaps, how much I dreaded the daily climb of the rigging, especially in a high sea, and the hand on the shoulder loosened its grip and gave a light pat. 'You do that, boy,' he said. 'We wouldn't be here without you, you know.'

I *did* know, but I didn't want Captain Smollett to guess how much Jim had told me of him and his friends. So I looked up at him without saying a word, and wondered if he would believe my apparent innocence. '*I* wouldn't be here without *you*, Captain,' I was beginning to say, when Joyce and Hunter, two of the Squire's men who had been on the first voyage out, ran up and said the tanks in the hold had all crashed and broken, and that fresh water and glass were swilling about everywhere. 'Permission to seal off the passage-way, Cap'n?' said Joyce.

'There's bleeding feet already,' Hunter added.

Captain Smollett frowned. 'Our tanks for the specimens gone,' he said in an angry voice. 'This isn't good for us. No, it's turning against us, this trip.' He signalled to the Squire, who was standing by the rail where Jim and I had stood and was staring down at the ocean.

It occurred to me I'd never seen such ham acting or not since my grandmother made me go to *Peter Pan* with her and I had to sit through Captain Hook rolling his eyes and pretending he wanted to kill young boys. It was for my benefit of course but this simple, plant-collecting expedition was beginning to seem like something that same poor grandmother of mine would have believed.

'Squire, we've lost our tanks. Of all things!' And he marched over to him, setting me free at last. 'We'll have to go back for replacements,' he said, before Dr Livesey came up to join them at the rail and blocked out the conversation with his high, sloping back.

Squire Trelawney nodded vigorously, and soon I could see Dr Livesey's head jerking up and down, like a puppet on a string.

But when the Captain walked sharply past me on his way to the bridge – and Admiral Guinea was standing there nodding, too – I could hardly stop myself from smiling.

Go back? For tanks that would never have held more than a pretence of the reason for the journey to Treasure Island? I knew for sure then, and I was glad they didn't know I knew, that the Captain would never turn back. They were after treasure and they wouldn't let even the oil slick stand in their way.

CHAPTER NINE

Morning brought an even higher wind and a sky mottled with clouds under which we raced in the wrong direction.

The oil slick, visible from the crow's nest and occupying more sea miles than I would have liked to tell Captain Smollett about, made a great 'S' round us. When I climbed down to the bridge, I was told to draw out the shape of the slick on a piece of paper and, as I did so, Captain Smollett's face darkened. 'We'll be years in this enterprise,' he said. 'If you can see so much, boy, can't you see a way out of it?'

'We could risk following it up to the top – ' (by this I meant the horizon, which swallowed the brown path made by the oil, and took it out of sight altogether) 'instead of losing ground, sir.'

Captain Smollett looked at me sharply. He must have realized I knew we weren't returning for replacements for the water-tanks, although we were going back on our tracks in order to avoid the oil. 'But if we can't cross it,' the Captain snapped, 'we'll end up in Iceland!'

Nevertheless, he gave orders to go about again, and we followed the slick, which was a dangerous and frightening thing to do, not to mention all the responsibility being on me to keep us clear of disaster. I don't think I ever felt so tired in my life and, that night, when the course for the following hours had been charted, I fell straight into my hammock. (I was on deck, now, in the companion-way, beside Captain Smollett) and slept without a dream.

After some days came the second of the unforeseen happenings which were to change our course – and this time with more far-reaching consequences than before. I was to see how dull our crew were, and how incapable of dealing with an emergency.

I was in the crow's nest as usual, bleary-eyed from short nights and the strain of looking out at the treacherous movements of the oil slick. Jim stood on deck directly below. From time to time he looked up and gave a friendly wave – he was much easier to get on with now he no longer had to pretend that the reason for our journey was other than the finding of more treasure. We even managed, in the early mornings before I had to climb up to my post, to laugh together over the worried faces of Squire Trelawney and Captain Smollett as they daily watched the *Hispaniola* forced north by the passage of oil.

Jim was in the middle of one of these arm-wavings when I saw him swing round suddenly and race over to the rail. He pointed and he shouted something, but the wind blew his words away. I stared out to sea. And I gripped the sides of my narrow perch when I saw what was coming at us or bearing up on us, rather, from under the grey, monotonous swell.

A submarine was flying through the water and making to cut us off across the bows. It came at such speed that it was alongside before I had time even to scramble down the rigging and shout the alarm. I could see her name, painted in tall letters on the hull, *Revenge*.

Squire Trelawney and Admiral Guinea seized hold of me as I touched down. The Squire looked bad enough, with his wig slipped to one side and his normally jovial face grey and purple in patches. But Admiral Guinea was literally demented. He put his face down to mine and then gobbled, like a turkey. 'Why didn't you *see* –' the Squire shouted, when it became clear Admiral Guinea couldn't get the words out. 'What is it, boy? What in the name of the devil *is* it?'

'A dolphin,' Jim called out as he ran towards us. 'I saw it first, Squire.' And he laughed like a young child at having tricked me at my high post over the sea.

It was clear, I suddenly saw, that machines from my own time could be seen by the others if they mistook them for natural phenomena. One of these days they'd see a 'bird' in the sky and there would be their first plane but perhaps there was something too rigid about the wings to take them in like that. At any rate, I'd seldom heard Jim give so joyous a laugh as when he saw his 'dolphin' coming up through the water.

It was my turn to laugh, though, when I saw the expression on Captain Smollett's face. After he had finished berating the crew for noticing nothing (and indeed it was their job to see an underwater monster, not mine) he turned back to the mysterious dolphin and his mouth fell open as if a hand tugged at his jaw. 'No . . . no . . .' he muttered. 'It can't be, boy . . .' and he stumbled in my direction, seeking reassurance. I could see that the scene presenting itself to port of our bows was an impossible miracle to Captain Smollett and his friends. And for a moment I stared in astonishment myself.

Rain and sun, together in a brief interlude from the raging wind, had gone down into the sea and pulled out of it an arch of misty colours – a sea-bow which framed the metal dolphin bobbing in the waves. In that film of colours it was easy to believe that none other than a mermaid was rising slowly from the dolphin's back – that we had been visited by a siren, who would lure us with her singing on to the rocks. I knew, of course, that it was a periscope which had risen out of the water, and that a real woman's head and chest were coming up out of the hatch. Yet, as I say, I stood amazed for a few seconds at the miracles modern science can achieve.

Admiral Guinea was by now almost beside himself with rage and fear. 'Arethusa,' he cried, staggering against the rail and then pitching back into the boom, 'go away, Arethusa!'

I must admit, this chilled me a good deal. I'd dreamed of Arethusa, cast out cruelly by her father, of her misery and grief, as Blind Pew had told that night at the *Benbow* inn. How many years had she languished, waiting for the sailor the Admiral had sent away? I saw the word *Revenge* again, on the shining snout of the submarine, and I saw us all blown to pieces, torpedoed, before Captain Smollett had uselessly given orders to go about.

The submarine was right alongside now, and the tall, black-haired figure of Arethusa swung up on to the deck of the *Hispaniola*, without anyone daring to challenge her right to do so.

She was a terrifying sight. She was so tall the Squire seemed dwarfed beside her. Her hair was as wet and black as seaweed. Her big black eyes were ringed with white, like the eyes of a dead body that's been a long time in the sea. And her lips (perhaps it was the light from the sea-bow, which still flickered behind her) were a vicious green. 'Father!' she said.

This monstrous apparition strode towards us, and I must say we all shrank away. 'It's good to see you again, father!' A hand came out but not in greeting. I saw a Black Spot in the palm of the hand.

'Arethusa – what do you want?' Then Guinea, when he saw what had been passed to him, turned, if possible,

an even deeper red in the face than before. 'You've got the mutineers with you, Arethusa –' he gasped out, as he saw a line of men clambering up on to deck. 'Away with them – let them hang and sun-dry – I knew I was right to cast you out, Arethusa!' And Admiral Guinea gave a terrible shudder as if he was about to drop dead there and then at the foot of the mast.

Squire Trelawney showed equal horror at the progression of pirates coming aboard. 'Israel Hands!' he cried out. 'Job Anderson! Arethusa, are you the leader of these vagabonds?'

Arethusa turned and smiled a green smile at him. 'I am, Squire. And we have a power that will take you to that island of yours at a greater speed than you might imagine.' She pointed down with a long hand at the submarine, the hard fish at which crew and Captain alike still boggled. 'We will take you there. In return for that map, dear Squire – or we will blow you to pieces!'

This was just what I had feared. Squire Trelawney, however, paid little attention to this: he was obviously unaware of the type of missile Arethusa would be carrying in the belly of her fish. 'And Long John Silver,' he said, 'where is that rascal, among these gentlemen of fortune here?'

Arethusa burst out laughing. Her teeth, black stumps capped with gold, shone like treasure buried in earth. 'Long John Silver, my dear Squire Trelawney? If he were here with me, d'you think I'd come proposing a partnership to find the treasure?'

'A partnership?' said Dr Livesey, stepping forward and

speaking for the first time. I saw him look round the *Hispaniola* at the mutineers, and Captain Smollett, and the crew standing like a school of porpoises, and then at Jim and me, out by the roundhouse and as far as we could be from Admiral Guinea and his terrible daughter.

'Yes.' Arethusa spoke to Dr Livesey now as if he were the only man with any courage on the ship. 'You'll surely remember that Long John Silver hopped ashore on the journey back from Treasure Island, when you put in at New Mexico. Or so I've often been told,' and here she glared in a particularly menacing way at Admiral Guinea. 'Told by a father who was a slaver, a killer of men –'

'No! Arethusa, stop!' pleaded the old Admiral.

'And a seeker for treasure,' she went on. 'He befriended *you* –' and she glared again at Squire Trelawney, 'because he was in possession of a map! Captain Flint's first map with the most important treasure of all marked on it. Father,' she swung down on him with long strides, and although the *Hispaniola* was pitching and tossing in the high seas, her step never faltered, '*you* shipped with Flint the pirate! Only you and Long John Silver know where that treasure lies! And Silver's gone –'

A mass of voices broke out then. The crew, associating Admiral Guinea with their Captain and the Squire, were shocked to find themselves taken on by a band of treasure-hunters. The Captain and Trelawney were discussing their new situation rapidly. Only Dr Livesey (who was a sensible man, I have to confess, and a doctor like my father) went over to Arethusa and had the nerve to stand right up to her, although his head came only to her shoulder. 'We accept the partnership,' he said, 'if we can take our share in the treasure.' Arethusa smiled down at him. 'You shall have your share in the treasure,' she said. Then she looked up suddenly and saw us – Jim and me – with our heads sticking out from behind the roundhouse. 'And who is *that*?' she cried, pointing straight at me.

Dr Livesey turned, too, and when he saw me his face creased in a smile, which reminded me even more of my father when he was trying to reassure a patient. 'That, ma'am, is our . . . our ship's boy. And a very useful boy, too, I may say. He can see the future, with your permission, ma'am.'

I don't think Silver himself could ever have been as oily and obsequious as Dr Livesey was just then. But the effect of the speech on Arethusa was quite different from what he must have expected. 'You can, can you, boy?' she said in a quiet, strange voice. And those long strides came over the deck, this time in the direction of the roundhouse.

Powerful arms swept me up. Hands and Job Anderson passed me down the hatch into the submarine before I could give even a backward glance to Jim.

And that is how I found myself in a submarine, racing under water to Treasure Island, with the *Hispaniola* pulled along in our wake by its invisible steed.

CHAPTER TEN

Inside the submarine was the strangest jumble of past and present I had ever set eyes on. Even if I did feel I'd walked into a James Bond film, I was too excited to be afraid. I just wished Jim could be there, to see for the first time the magnificent panel of controls, the gleaming radar screens and fields of multi-coloured switches in the computer-bank. And when I saw the expert way the mutineers, tough men who looked as if they'd sailed a hundred times to Treasure Island, handled the complex machinery, I couldn't help feel sorry for the poor crew of the *Hispaniola*. What a long way mankind had come in the past couple of centuries – or had they? For these men were just as much pirates as they had ever been. They were more powerful now, that was all: masters of weapons and knowledge that could blast us all into outer space.

I didn't have much time for these thoughts, though, for Arethusa marched me away from the control room and down a narrow corridor into what must have been her private boudoir (if that can be the word for a pirate leader's den). 'Tell me, boy,' she said, while I stood staring round me wide-eyed, 'tell me how you came to be on the *Hispaniola*, with that devil, my father.'

At first I couldn't reply. The contrast with the other part of the submarine was too great, and I felt as if I had been spirited back again, to an age of distant finery, where the growl from the powerful engines could only be the roar of wind on the sea.

Striped silk hangings, such as I had seen in pictures of ancient Bedouin tents, covered the walls. Elephant tusks, crossed like great scimitars, were ranged over them. On the floor were piles of cushions – tapestry cushions, cushions embossed with strange flowers – and low tables, inlaid with mother-of-pearl. And on the wall behind Arethusa, who had seated herself on the only chair – a gold throne in the form of a scallop, with precious stones rising above her head in a fan – hung a parrot in a cage. The cage was jewelled, too, and this made the parrot's feathers look all the more dim and mouldy. I couldn't help thinking that of all the strange, old things in the room, the bird must be the oldest by far.

'You haven't answered me,' Arethusa said in an impatient tone. 'And tell me about these special powers you're supposed to have. And quickly!'

'Oh . . . I . . .' I stopped, and began to feel the fear my curiosity had kept away. 'I don't see the future or, rather, only *their* future,' I stuttered. 'You see, they needed me at the look-out in case of collision . . .' Then, my curiosity getting the better of me again, I burst out, 'How is it *you* can manage these things – things like submarines – when they've never so much as seen one?'

'Never you mind.' Arethusa was staring at me fiercely, and I could sense her disappointment. Had she really imagined I could look into the future, the years after my own death? 'I'll tell you,' she said suddenly, and her voice was softer now, as if she realized I could be of

no use to her, and therefore not worth interrogating with harshness. 'After I was thrown out of home by my father – and for the simple crime of wanting to marry – I travelled the world for many years. And on these travels I met a man – a doctor – who offered me the possibility of revenge. He would give me life – until such time as my revenge was completed – and all the sophistications of the changing world to achieve it, if I could bring him the treasure he had wanted so long.'

'The treasure?' I said stupidly. And the parrot behind Arethusa said, 'The treasure, the treasure, Cap'n Flint's Treasure,' so that I jumped nearly out of my skin.

'Yes,' Arethusa said quietly. 'The treasure my father wants so desperately to find. The treasure everyone has wanted since the beginning of time –'

Here she had to break off. The door of the den opened with a bang and Israel Hands fell in, on to the cushions. At the same time, bells went off in the submarine and there was a commotion of people running and shouting. The lights went out and then came on again, while the parrot madly flapped its wings in the cage. 'Reef!' Israel Hands shouted. 'Going up!' And he dashed out of the door, to swear in the passage as he ran against the other mutineers rushing to their leader's den.

Arethusa smiled her black-and-gold smile. And I shuddered again for horror of her, just as I had begun to feel pity for her predicament. 'They're excitable, despite all the modern technology,' she said. 'But if we were close to coming aground on a reef, I'd say we were in Caribbean waters already. Wouldn't you, boy?'

I didn't know what to say, so I kept silent. The great female pirate pointed to a cushion and swept out of the den. 'Sleep there, boy. You'll need all the rest you can get for the morning.' And she pulled the door shut behind her.

'Cap'n Flint's Treasure,' said the parrot again and again but I soon slept.

CHAPTER ELEVEN

It's difficult to tell what time it is when you're buried in
a capsule under the sea, so I don't know how many days
passed or how many nights I slept, so strange were the
dreams that came to me. And it was hard enough to tell
them from the exotic cabin and the intricate designs of the
tapestries where I lay.

Arethusa visited from time to time, I think, and soft
lights came on at intervals, when I was brought food that
was scented and delicious and quite unlike anything I
had tasted before. Bells rang occasionally and steps
sounded. Then, one day (it was night in my little den)
old Job Anderson poked his head round the door and
told me we were there. 'There?' The food and drink had
been drugged, perhaps. I couldn't even remember where
I was going, or why.

Anderson grabbed my arm and propelled me along the
passage to the chute. 'And you're the one she wants to go
and get the map,' he hissed in my ear as he pushed me
again, this time upward. 'Hurry now!'

There would certainly have been something the matter
with me if I hadn't known where I was – or why – when
I looked out from the height of the submarine hatch at
my new surroundings.

The *Hispaniola* lay directly behind us, sails furled. She
showed no sign, I thought, of the unnatural speed at

66

which she had crossed the Atlantic: the paint on the hull was fresh, the brass nine amidships gleamed in the sun.

Before us lay Treasure Island. It must have been very early morning for a violet-coloured cloud, a remnant of tropical night, hung over Spyglass Hill and the water was so pale a blue it looked like glass.

The next thing I realized was that there was no one visible on the *Hispaniola* and no one audible below me in the submarine. It was as if the whole place was holding its breath, and waiting for me to make the first move.

A dinghy was secured to the side of the submarine. I slid down into it and untied the rope. My paddle went through the still water without ar.y sound. It was ghostly, paddling to a ship with a cargo of people who could only see the submarine because they thought it was a dolphin, or a whale. And I didn't like the silence, off the coast of that island, where a new moon hung in the sky over dawn clouds the colour of flamingoes.

The silence ended, though. As my little boat bumped up against the *Hispaniola* a clatter of feet sounded on deck, and a shot rang out. A great flock of birds rose up out of the trees, and flew over us, to circle in the sky and return in a black swarm to Captain Kidd's Anchorage. This made mc more nervous than before and I crouched in the bottom of the dinghy, praying I could wake and find myself safely home again. I hated Treasure Island then, and I knew nothing but bad would come of it.

'Boy!'

Admiral Guinea was leaning over the rail, and I could

see he was holding the old parchment map in his hand. 'Up the side, boy!'

When I reached the deck I saw Jim was there, and Squire Trelawney, Captain Smollett and Dr Livesey. Redruth and the crew stood behind – and not one of them smiled in welcome when they saw me arrive.

Squire Trelawney stepped forward. 'This is very important, boy, so listen properly.' I nodded, though I felt he expected me to salute, so strict was his tone of voice. 'You take this map to Arethusa.' The Squire reached out to Admiral Guinea who unfolded the parchment. 'You see this red X, here in the south, you tell her that's where the treasure's buried, and you go with her party, to the south here, you understand?' He tapped the parchment repeatedly with his thumb. 'Now off you go, boy.' And he practically shoved me on to the companion-way.

I don't know if it was the tapping noise of his thumb on the parchment which brought back the memory of old Pew tapping down the passage of the *Benbow* inn and his voice, saying to Admiral Guinea, 'Where Cap'n Flint put it, Admiral –' 'But the treasure's in the north, sir,' I blurted out, in that awful habit I had. And as I spoke, I remembered the map spread on the table in the Captain's cabin, too, with the fiery cross in the north, at the mouth of the north inlet, to be precise.

It wasn't long before I wished I hadn't spoken. A hand shot out – Admiral Guinea's this time – and dragged me back on deck. 'Now look, boy,' Admiral Guinea's dark, weatherbeaten face looked down into mine. I couldn't help thinking that was how he'd look if he were hanged, and 'sun-dried' as the mutineers nicely put it. And no doubt he deserved to be for he went on, in what he imagined to be a persuasive, cajoling tone, 'It's like this, lad. Don't you pay any attention whatsoever to that woman Arethusa. She's mad — you can see that, can't you? Are you old enough to see that, eh? I wouldn't be surprised if she hasn't filled your mind with all manner of foolish stories — being thrown out by her father for wanting to marry a privateersman, cruelty stories — the whole brigful of 'em.' And Admiral Guinea clamped his hand down on me so that I felt like a piece of skinned meat about to be hung up to dry in the halyards. 'What *did* she tell you, boy? It was that husband of hers came with Pew one night to *rob* me — kill me, most likely. And now she fills your head with lies! Speak up, boy, and come out with it!'

I couldn't tell Admiral Guinea or the Doctor of Arethusa's revenge and her plan for the treasure. At the same time I couldn't help feeling she *was* mad — that this important treasure, whatever it was, would come to no good in her hands. As I stood there, perplexed, Admiral Guinea gave a loud, jeering laugh, as if to show he'd persuaded me of his daughter's madness for once and for all.

And, obligingly, Squire Trelawney and Captain Smollett — and even Jim — burst out laughing on deck behind us. I must say I was tempted to agree with Admiral Guinea if I hadn't heard Blind Pew's catalogue of his crimes that night at the inn. But to go back to the submarine and trick Arethusa with a false map – that was unthinkable, too. 'You see this here,' Admiral Guinea's hand, veined and crossed as the map, dangled the parchment before me. 'Cross the swamp and you're there.'

I had to own that the map looked very convincing – I wondered if it had been Dr Livesey, with his neat hands, who had concocted it.

Admiral Guinea threw back his head and laughed, which wasn't a pleasant sight. 'That mad-minded daughter of mine – well, she thinks Long John Silver brought the treasure back to the same spot where he found it, after he jumped ship in New Mexico on the voyage home. That fool of a half-woman, with all those high and mighty airs, she actually *considers*,' and here Admiral Guinea spat vigorously over the taffrail, 'that Silver would do a thing like that! She worships the memory of the old sea-cook, you know. "If I'd been born a boy I'd have been Silver," she used to say.' But the Admiral's eyes didn't soften at this point. 'Do you think,' he hissed at me suddenly, 'that Silver would've gone back to that spot, where any marauder would go? No, he knew the correct position of the real treasure – he'd served with Flint, remember. But you take her to the south!' Here Guinea gave me one of his famous shoves and I nearly plunged into the water. 'Tell her it's buried under the tallest tree, just as it was before!' And he gave another of his mast-shaking laughs.

None of this made much sense to me. I thought back to the treasure under the tallest tree, in the book I had read so often that, at night, that tree used to stand up outside my window, dark against the sky with the booty of a thousand pirates buried under its roots.

But I could see, from the grim faces of Squire Trelawney and Captain Smollett that the time for laughter was over, and that I must obey without losing a moment more. 'You double-cross us and you'll swing from there,' said Admiral Guinea, pointing up to the crow's nest where I had spent so many lonely hours. Then he had the kindness to add, as I was allowed finally down to the dinghy, 'And you can dodge back and join us here for the return. But you've got to be quick – as we'll be – and we'll be the only ones off the island.'

So that was the plan. Arethusa and the mutineers were to be marooned while searching in the south of the island. It would be Admiral Guinea's revenge, after all. I couldn't help thinking, as I paddled over that eerily quiet stretch of water, that Admiral Guinea might feel quite differently when his daughter, enraged by his trick, caught up with him and blew him to smithereens with the missiles from the submarine. And if the Admiral thought he could easily destroy 'the dolphin' before leaving the island, he would again find it a harder task than he had thought.

So, it was with a sinking heart that I made my way to the submarine and clambered up to the hatch.

CHAPTER TWELVE

Now I look back on the search for 'Cap'n Flint's treasure' on the island, I wonder at the way Arethusa and her band of pirates were so effortlessly duped by the Admiral's false map.

Arethusa was waiting, eyes rolling impatiently. The parrot, released from its cage, was flapping on her shoulder. No sooner had I handed over the map than she ordered us all out double-quick, and in a convoy of dinghies we reached the shore.

Nor did she appear surprised at Captain Smollett sending Jim in a longboat to deliver the message that she should go ahead and the others would follow shortly. I suppose her desire to reach the spot was greater than caution and, also, by keeping Jim in our party, she knew she had a hostage in case of foul play. Nevertheless, it was I who was surprised by the casual way she strode off, parrot and all, into the trees, leaving us to catch up with her as best we could.

In the last half-hour the heat had grown intense and the violet cloud over the island had melted away. The black birds rose again in a terrible clatter – and this set off the parrot, who cried 'Cap'n Flint's treasure.' Then, as we came out into a clearing by the swamp with the new moon, very pale now, still hanging over us in the sky, it shrieked 'New Moon, Old Moon,' until my head ached and the birds flew off in alarm. I was too full of thoughts to wonder how this ancient parrot of Arethusa could have the intelligence to see the moon was new, but the maddening cry certainly made it harder still to work out how I could escape the terrifying situation I was in.

The mutineers ran with great agility over the swamp, never pausing long enough to sink into the green slime. As for Arethusa, her tall figure seemed to fly ahead of us. We were soon in a forest of much taller trees – they'd been tall enough, I remembered, at the time of the first visit to the island and they'd had centuries to grow even higher since – and I began to recognize the scene of Ben Gunn's haunting of the pirates. The great tree, high above us, I could see at once as the place of the burial of the first treasure and then I saw Arethusa stop, and look down in a frenzied way at the map, as she tried to make out the exact spot of Captain Flint's hiding-place.

This was my chance. I wanted, at that point, only to escape, to seize the submarine if I could, and pray for guidance that I would understand the workings of the controls. I would race underwater to the shores of England and then go up the cliff behind the *Admiral Benbow* inn. Then I'd run all the way over the fields to my father and mother's house and there'd be no Blind Pew this time to tap-tap behind me as I went. I can say I didn't have high hopes of succeeding. But there was no other way out. I wanted nothing to do with either party on Treasure Island, the wicked Admiral Guinea or his equally wicked daughter. If I vanished now, no one would notice in the excitement, especially with Jim still there.

A shout rang out. I couldn't think at once that it came from Arethusa; it sounded more like an angry dog, howling at the moon.

The 'new' red X on the map had led the pirates to a spot some 400 metres from the tall tree. As they fell back in disarray at the shout of rage from Arethusa, I saw the trick Admiral Guinea had played on his daughter and, for a fatal minute, I stood rooted to the spot, instead of running away.

Guinea – or a member of the crew sent by him – must have slipped out of the *Hispaniola* in the darkness before dawn. For the newly-marked 'tallest tree' was none other than a wooden leg – a reminder of Long John Silver, no doubt, a cruel joke and one calculated to bring that shout of rage from Arethusa.

Even Israel Hands stood abashed. The other pirates, stupefied probably by the years of rum and wandering the world in search of the treasure, went down like idiots on their hands and knees and started scrabbling in the earth. It wasn't long before even they could see there was no cavity under the turf and the pine needles, and that there never had been. In one rush they went to the tree where the treasure had lain that Squire Trelawney once so triumphantly claimed. But the hole, still empty, contained only moss and the other creeping visitors of the forest. Then they stood up and shouted, too, and the birds rose once more out of the trees behind us, while the parrot, rocking dementedly on Arethusa's shoulder, screamed 'New Moon' until the island trembled with noise.

I don't know if anyone saw me go. And I can't re-member how I dodged them, running through the trees and bearing always east in my attempt to get back to the submarine before they did. All I do know is that the

swamps and the monotonous forest misled me. In what seemed like the space of one tick of a clock and the next I had stumbled on the north inlet. I was out in the open, the cover of the trees was behind me, and I was witnessing another scene of rage, this time on the part of Admiral Guinea, Squire Trelawney and the other 'honest men' who had put to sea in the *Hispaniola*.

Clearly, there had once been a burial place at the spot of the true red X on Admiral Guinea's map. The ground, which Squire Trelawney and his men had dug rapidly with their spades, had fallen away at the attack, and an oblong hole lay exposed, about the size of a small tomb.

That there was nothing in it was plain from the shouts of anger and disappointment. Only Dr Livesey, as I saw from my dangerous vantage point, was silent and stood with lips pursed a few feet away from the rest. Even Captain Smollett was groaning aloud. And, as for Admiral Guinea, I don't need to describe the state he was in. 'Back to the ship!' the Squire was shouting. 'That devil Silver took it in the end! To New Mexico and we'll track him down. And before we're caught by the dolphin!'

Then he looked up and saw me. 'Boy!' his voice echoed across the narrow inlet. The others looked up as well. 'It's the boy,' yelled Captain Smollett, who was quite as excited as the Squire. 'They haven't got him! Quick, boy! Here!'

Whether they thought I was Jim, or whether they knew I was Sam – and they needed me to steer safely – I didn't have time to consider, as I ran back into the trees.

I knew only one thing: that they didn't have a chance in
hell, in the *Hispaniola*, with an angry Arethusa in her
submarine on their tail. If I joined them, I would die. So
I ran, faster than ever before, and this time to the west,
to the windward of the island, to hide until they were
gone. I didn't care that my fate would be as bad as poor
Ben Gunn's had been, marooned in that evilly quiet
place, with only berries to eat and the sound of the birds

clattering out of the trees. I wanted only to lie low, to be left in peace until all the treasure-seekers had left the island in its old oblivion.

The strangest thing is that, in the midst of all that turmoil, I was more scared by the absolute windlessness, the literal dead quiet in the shallow scoop of land where I found myself, than if I'd been right in the centre of a battle with the 'honest men'.

It was as if nothing had ever grown there except the low grass in vicious spikes that stuck up out of sand the colour of wet tea. The trees that stood in a circle were as forlorn as scarecrows after a century of motionless air: their branches drooped and they seemed to be guarding nothing although they stood around like sentinels.

Yet I was too tired by now to leave this haunted saucer of misery and I went to sit by one of the trees for a while to get my breath and, if possible, my bearings.

The scoop below me was like an amphitheatre from the days of ancient Greece – I half expected to see a cast of actors, walking on stilts, rise up out of the swampy ground and recite their lines. And what I *did* see was as ghostly, as spine-chilling, as any sudden visitation by the spirits of a long-dead past.

Slowly, noiselessly, Arethusa stepped into the circle of ground. There was no one with her. The black trees provided a menacing diadem to her head of black hair as she advanced to the centre of the circle and came to a halt.

What did she want – Arethusa, tricked by her wicked father, doubly traduced in a life-time, cheated of her revenge and her treasure, too, and the immortality promised by the great Doctor who had tried to use her for his own ends? What could this solitary visit mean when she should surely have been attacking the *Hispaniola*, taking advantage of all the modern technology she possessed to destroy her father and his company? Or had her power over the future been stripped already by the Doctor as a punishment for her failure to bring the treasure to him. Was the submarine simply a dolphin by now — a Cinderella's coach turned pumpkin at the stroke of her loss?

I couldn't know the answers, in this enchanted compound cut off from the island, from the rest of the world, by the crowding, mournful trees. I can only report that I saw an extraordinary transformation and that I clung to the lowest branches of the tree where I was hiding, even though they poked into my ribs like cruel fingers.

Down from the low hills behind the trees came a troupe of women pirates. I swear this is what I saw: I swear Arethusa came towards them in the guise of Long John Silver, that she was as nimble on her wooden leg as the old sea-cook had been and that her troupe of female mutineers waved their tattered cockaded hats and cried out in admiration for her.

I never saw such a bunch of women in my life. And some of them were only girls, with eye-patches, too, and a skull and crossbones tattooed on their arms. They surrounded the new 'Long John Silver' and carried her to a throne they had brought in the centre of the circle. When they had finished saluting and bowing, they sat cross-

legged around the rough bamboo throne, and I heard
their plan, though it made my blood run cold to think of
the number of lives lost that it would entail.

'We'll never let them get away with it,' Arethusa was
saying. 'We'll die first –'

'They'll die first,' cried a girl with yellow hair under a

red-spotted handkerchief. She looked more like a gypsy than a pirate, I thought. 'Show Long John the cannon, sisters! And quick!'

'We found it on the South Beach!' came a chorus of voices as the great old Spanish cannon was wheeled from behind the trees and into the circle. 'Must have been from a man o'war wrecked off the coast. And it *works*!'

At this, two old cannon-balls were produced; and from the distance I was, I could feel Arethusa 'Long John Silver' bounce with excitement.

'And do we have flint for firing the cannon?' she asked softly.

'Yes, ma'am, we do,' the pirates called back.

'Very well then. We'll blow up the *Hispaniola*.'

Arethusa's black eyes sparkled and it seemed, for a moment, that the black trees surrounding her bowed in deference, too, to her great rage.

'A flint, a flint,' she mused; then she burst out laughing. 'If we can't get Cap'n Flint's treasure, a flint to the cannon'll blow them all out of the water,' she said. 'If we don't bear it away, nobody does. Agreed?'

The shout of war from the Amazon group there was enough to dislodge me from my perch in the lowest branch of the tree. It sent me running further westward, as far as I could go from their cutlasses and their pounding feet, as they ran with the cannon up out of the circle with Arethusa, waving crutches, held aloft by them on her bamboo chair. I saw only death and blood ahead; I could hear in my mind the roar of the rusty old cannon as it blew the *Hispaniola* into matchwood. I felt I could see, too, a few pretty pirates' heads bobbing without bodies on the blood-stained blue of the sea.

Soon the sound of shouting died down and I was running on sandy soil, with the trees more widely spaced and glimpses of a rough, blue sea in between. My mind was in too much of a daze to wonder where that strange encampment of female pirates might live on the island, or how they had got there. They'd come over with Long John Silver, perhaps when he jumped ship in New Mexico and he'd abandoned them there to wait for his return. Nor did I ever discover, in all the terrifying events which lay in store on that benighted island, whether or not they survived to return to the trees from which they'd so suddenly appeared. Maybe they had really thought Arethusa was their lost leader but, as I raced away, it all seemed to add up to yet another fragment of a dream. And I was no longer sure whose dream I might be caught in now!

Eventually I came to a long strand, with hummocks covered in grass sloping down to the water, and there I collapsed, so short of breath I thought my heart would jump out of my chest, and more dead than alive, as I already knew.

CHAPTER THIRTEEN

My rest wasn't to last many minutes, on that beach where long waves rolled in and landed in a spew of foam before pulling out again, specked with the little, glittering leaves of manchineal that lay fallen on the sand. I didn't have time, either, to reflect that the real name of Treasure Island was still unknown to me or to curse the curiosity over 'Latitude and longitude struck out by J. Hawkins' that had led me to this: a castaway on an island where I would never be able to survive. I closed my eyes and opened them again each time a wave rolled towards me, like a wave of sleep. But I knew the island must be filled with fighting by now as Admiral Guinea and Arethusa met on their return. Behind the roar and thud of the waves I thought I heard cries, and shots ring out. Then the sea deafened everything.

The sun was blotted out for a moment and I sat up. I had a raging headache. Sand had penetrated my shirt and clung to my back. The sun was stronger than ever. Then I saw what it was that flew backwards and forwards over the beach.

Arethusa's parrot, its mangy green and red feathers even more faded-looking in the strong sunlight, was circling and swooping before me. It landed once, gave me a cruel look, and took off again. 'New Moon, Old Moon,' it shrieked, over the hiss of the sea, 'Cap'n Flint's treasure. New Moon, Old.' A terrible sadness

came to me as I thought that this evil bird would be my
only companion from now on. And I was about to
struggle to my feet, to run and find the Squire or
Arethusa – perhaps to be killed was preferable after all
to slow death on Treasure Island – when a succession of
shots sounded from a short way behind me, and I fell on
my back again.

Then there was silence, except for the roar of the surf.
'New Moon, Old Moon,' cried the parrot.

My heart pounded, then died down. In a nervous
spasm the big toe of my left foot began drawing in the
sand.

Eyes – I knew they were eyes – peered out from the
low hedge of manchineal trees at my back. I sat up, fast,
and pulled my legs under me to bound into flight.

My eyes and those other eyes – whoever they belonged to – must have seen it at the same time. On the smooth surface of the sand lay a new moon and an old moon etched by my big toe. They spelt the word C O C O. I jumped to my feet and started to run along the beach.

At the same time, there was a clatter in the bushes. A shot was fired – there was a sound of falling on prickly leaves – and then feet going at speed in the opposite direction to mine. But I just kept running. On that endless beach, which spread out in front of me like the yellow path the already-setting sun made from the water's edge to the rim of the sky, I ran as uselessly as a blowing leaf.

CHAPTER FOURTEEN

I suppose you could say it was the parrot who saved me – the parrot I had hated as it flew overhead and whose incessant cry of 'New Moon, Old Moon,' had led me to draw out, quite unthinkingly, the name of the island where Captain Flint's treasure must really be.

At the time, of course, I was in no state to think this out. All I knew, as I ran, was that a hill began to show itself in the distance – and I thought I was dreaming it sometimes, it seemed so far away and cloudy in the tropical twilight. I must get there, and I would find protection – but why I thought that isn't clear to me either, unless the straightness and emptiness of the beach were beginning to drive me mad.

In fact, the hill gave me more than protection, as it turned out. It gave me a view of the strangest and most horrifying scene I had ever witnessed. And I ran, panting, to the top, as if I knew I would be just in time.

The top of the hill was a plateau with the crest sliced off. For all my confusion, I realized I was on Spyglass Hill and as I crawled over the short, spiky grass I saw an inlet to the south of me and, to the east, the bulk of the island, going out as far as the leeward shore.

The battle was being waged on that shore.

I could make out the tall, gaunt figure of Arethusa. It was harder to pick out the men but Admiral Guinea it certainly was who lunged forward with a pistol and someone (Captain Smollett? Dr Livesey?) rushed up from behind Arethusa's group of mutineers and fired.

All hell broke out. The sun was going rapidly and I could see the shot burn red in the greying sky over the *Hispaniola*. Shouts and yells rose and then vanished, wiped away by the sea below Spyglass Hill on the windward side. I could no longer make out Arethusa – whether she had fallen or run for cover – or Guinea, even, in the darkness not yet lit by moon or stars. But I heard the splash of bodies as they hit the water. Whether they were dead or swimming for their lives, it was impossible to tell. The answer came soon enough.

Suddenly, in a burst of light, the submarine lay illumined in the black water. The roar of the old cannon rang out – and a terrible yell of pain – and a cry of triumph in a woman's voice that was as terrible as the death-cry a moment before.

I never imagined Arethusa would lose her head to the extent of blowing a man to smithereens when all she had to do was wait until the *Hispaniola* had its full capacity of passengers and catch the lot in one go, sending the three-masted schooner and the three-cornered hats into the black, clear depths of the Caribbean sea.

But I learned that night that the desire for revenge (alas for our doomed race) is stronger than any other.

Arethusa saw her father on the narrow beach of the natural harbour where his ship and her 'dolphin' were at anchor – and it was her father she wanted to kill.

She could have held back, as the troupe of Amazons must have been urging her to do, while Guinea paddled out in the dinghy to the ship. She would have had to wait, as every stroke of the oar went into the water, tapping the surface of the sea like a crippled man going off into the distance – like Long John Silver, disappearing again and this time for good, skimming the sea with a wooden paddle for a leg. There would have been silence, and then the faint plash of a wave against the *Hispaniola*, made by the Admiral's clumsy attempts to board.

Instead, frightened as well perhaps by the sudden lighting-up of the submarine – by some drunken fool left behind there to guard it, no doubt – Arethusa had fired the cannon straight at Admiral Guinea on the beach.

The shout of agony must have been his; the yell of triumph hers.

In the doorway of light from the submarine I then saw something else I had never expected to see. Arethusa was kneeling over the body of her father. She was sobbing.

Out of the shadows of the gloomy trees that came down to the sand the Amazons crept to comfort her. They made a strange circle in that hot, velvety night where the submarine lay like a furnace ready to be fired, on sea as flat and glittering as metal. They huddled in round Guinea and his daughter – and, all the while, my heart was in my mouth for footsteps must have been growing closer in those trees and the battle to the death was surely at hand.

From my distant vantage point, I couldn't make out who the shadowy figures were that shot out on to the beach at the speed of ferrets and ran for the cannon. In the lull in the fighting, caused by Arethusa's terrifying, pounding shot, some of the *Hispaniola* crew, unable to reach the water and swim for the ship, must have darted back under the trees for cover, I suppose – and now only too easily saw their opportunity.

There was one piece of munition left, I knew. And I knew I must board the *Hispaniola* and get away – before the outcome of the struggle that had now resumed on the beach could be decided, before the last piece of munition was fired either destroying the vessel of the dying father, Guinea, or the diving bird of his miserable daughter. I started to run. But before I was halfway down the hill I knew I was too late.

I heard the cannon go off – and, worse, I could have sworn that just before the explosion there came the sound of the Admiral's laugh. For a second of madness, as I ran blindly through the scrub, it seemed to me that Admiral Guinea must be immortal, impossible to kill. Or were the really evil people in this world always alive, whatever revenge was taken on them?

No doubt it was easy for the shadow-men from the *Hispaniola* to seize the cannon and turn it on the bright target in the water – but even though I could see what was coming, the blowing-up of the submarine seemed in its interminable, horrifying blast to be as close as you could get to the end of the world.

A ball of fire shot into the sky. The sound of the great bang echoed round the island. Then the flames went down and crept over the water, in a runway of tall flares, to the *Hispaniola*. The night was broken only by the sound of those birds, first disturbed by our arrival that morning, as they rose from the trees and metallically flapped their wings.

The flames went nearly to the *Hispaniola*. Then they stopped. The spillage of fuel from the submarine must have ended there, I suppose, and, as a result of my efforts, the *Hispaniola* was free of oil on her hull. I waited. Then voices came across the water.

It was hardly believable that anyone could have survived that holocaust but they had by jumping, perhaps, into the shallow water of Captain Kidd's Anchorage from the blast of the cannon-ball or, maybe, they'd been in the water all along and safe from the impact of the blast.

At any rate, they had. I stared in amazement. I ran but it was too late. As the moon rose over the Island and the sails began to draw, the *Hispaniola* eased her way out into the open sea. 'Coco Island,' called out a voice, belonging no doubt to whoever had spied on me on the beach!

And a joyful, boyish voice (I could have sworn it belonged to Jim) called back, 'Away to Cape Horn!'

I stood there, half-way down Spyglass Hill, and I heard furious sobs break out of my chest.

I was properly marooned this time. In the morning, no doubt, I would find myself alone with a collection of corpses and an exploded submarine. I went down the rest of the way slowly, hardly caring if I sank into the swamp by the mouth of the inlet.

And I thought I heard, very faintly wafting across the water:

> 'It's time for us to go —
> It's time for us to go — '

It's funny how things happen at times when there's no way out at all – when you've stopped wishing for them, even – and don't happen at those other times when it seems they've a reasonable chance of happening.

I almost walked right into the little boat which lay hidden in the reeds by a cave at the side of the water.

My mind must have been working fast, too, because I said aloud, 'It's the coracle.' And I stepped in and pushed off.

I knew, somehow, too, that Ben Gunn had never managed to get back to the island, although he'd hated his job as a steward in England when he was 'rescued' by the Squire on the first voyage. I didn't expect him to run from the cave in his beard and tattered coat. It didn't surprise me when no sound came from the birds as I nosed the coracle out into the mainstream. It was like movement in a dream. And there was no sign of Captain Flint's parrot, either, crying the name of the real island of treasure as I went.

The moon was high to the windward and the long, rolling waves passed under the coracle without threatening to swamp us. I lay on my stomach – as Jim had once done in the coracle – but this time with a patched old sail swelling above me. The last of a slab of bread and cheese I'd taken from the *Hispaniola* that morning came out of my pocket reluctantly, as it was stuck there with sand and seawater. I ate it as slowly as I could.

In spite of the extreme danger I was in, on the high seas in a coracle at night, I couldn't help smiling to myself.

For my thoughts, working in that strange way, had taken me back to school and the atlas I had yawned over so many times, and the sound of the teacher's voice, 'The Panama Canal. Sam, you're not paying attention! The Albatross basin. The Galapagos islands, where the earliest forms of life, discovered by Darwin . . .'

And I can see on the map, in my mind's eye, Coco Island just to the south of the Galapagos. 'A silly name for an island,' I'd said then.

The Panama Canal! How could the Squire or Captain Smollett or Arethusa, for that matter, if she was still alive, know of it, when they couldn't see beyond their own time? Arethusa would be powerless without her submarine. The Squire and Admiral Guinea, just aware of the discoveries of the age in which they had come to light, had pretended they were after this 'unknown' species. But they didn't know where it was or how to get there. I smiled, as the little coracle glided to the isthmus, at the thought of that party of treasure-seekers on their interminable way down to Cape Horn and up again on the far coast of South America. And I knew I was right to head for the canal: Treasure Island was generally considered to be somewhere in the Grenadines, or the Windward islands, to the east of the coast of South America. Now the first treasure was known to be a whole continent away, a tiny island lying on the Albatross basin of the west coast. By cutting through the Panama Canal I would arrive literally months ahead of the others!

After a while, I slept. I woke from time to time to see the ghostly banks of the canal on either side of me. It was like floating down a country lane while lying on your stomach over water. And I remembered the strange dream I'd had in the *Benbow* inn, of the scaly lid that came down on me as I tried to escape. This must have been the first sign of the part of the ocean I would eventually arrive at: the giant tortoise, first inhabitant of that ancient world.

Now I no longer knew what I would find there. Not the gold, I thought, which still haunted the minds of the Squire and mutineers alike. But something stranger — something unknown to the age I lived in — although it seemed impossible to imagine that anything unknown still existed in the world.

I slept again and when I woke properly it was to find the sun high in the sky. The sea was calm and so translucent that I could see swarms of brilliantly coloured fish in the water, hundreds of metres down. I sat up, stiff from sleep, and crawled under the sail for shade.

The island lay just ahead of us. It was true that it *did* resemble Jim Hawkins's island, only it was smaller and there were no trees. Otherwise, that second hill to the south of Spyglass Hill — which I had thought, looking at Admiral Guinea's map, could only have been a worn-away dune — was standing in place. Captain Flint had been right and Admiral Guinea had been right to insist that his map was the right one.

The coracle drifted into a small natural harbour and beached on shingle. Still hardly able to believe my luck, I stepped out.

Treasure Island! I was there!

CHAPTER SIXTEEN

At first I walked carefully. I imagined every hummock to be a giant tortoise and I thought I saw scorpions – in the strange, swaying dance I had watched on television at home – perched on each blade of grass.

But it didn't take long to realize there was no life on the island at all.

I was alone, really alone for the first time in my life. No birds rose with a clattering of wings as I went. No footsteps sounded after me as Pew's had done when the old scarecrow creaked in the wind. There was no wind, either, in this island bare of life.

I was at the north inlet before I knew it. Stagnant green water seeped in from a shore that looked as if it had been denuded of life, too, and violently. A crater about fifteen metres in perimeter took the place of the beach. Piles of dead coral, like the skeletons of animals, lay scattered around it. To the west of the crater, invisible from the little harbour where I had landed in my coracle, stood a single tree.

The tree was tall, taller than the tallest tree on Jim's island. It was bare, too, except for two branches sticking out at the top and I thought, for one mad moment, that a ship had grounded there and this was the mast.

I made my way over the swampy ground to the side of the green water. I walked up to the tree. There was no mistaking that this was where the red X on the map had been and no sign either of anything to find. I stopped and stood looking around me at the desolate scene.

Then I saw it. At the foot of the tree lay a shell. It was like a piece of tortoise-shell, but the colours weren't tortoise-shell colours: they were brighter, reds and

purples and greens that could never have come from the sea. It was longer, too, than any shell I'd seen in a museum at home. At one end was a round hole, about the size of a piece of eight but whether there had once been a gold coin in it would have been hard to say.

I bent down and picked up the shell. And I looked around again, guiltily, as if someone must be watching me. On this island where life had been so definitely stamped out, no sound came and no stirring, from water, grass or sand.

What happened then I still can't really believe. I lifted the round peep-hole to my eyes. It fitted exactly with the shell slipping over my face like a mask. I peered out.

Long John Silver stood before me. His round, smooth face beamed into mine. He leant on a crutch with one arm and, with the other, he propped himself against the tree. 'Well, boy!' he said. And he pointed up to the sky. 'You've come for the treasure. So look – and it's yours!'

I lifted my face upward. I gasped. And all I remember, as the sky turned black, is the sound of Silver's laughter, and my own head hitting the ground with a bang as loud and terrible as Arethusa's exploding submarine.

The future opened up to me. I don't doubt that, now I'm at home and in bed again and my mother has just come up the stairs to say I shall certainly be going to school tomorrow.

I saw the worlds – the worlds we know as little of now as Squire Trelawney and Captain Smollett knew of our world today.

But these worlds, which floated an infinite distance away in space and were still so close that I felt I could lift my hand up to them, were quite unlike the planet where I and Jim Hawkins could still recognize ourselves.

Every form of life was there. From the amoeba world, which split and re-formed in a million galaxies before my enchanted eye, to the world of the crustacean and the reptile, and then those mythical worlds of unicorns and salamanders, dead as the poor Pacific islands blown apart by man – all were there, and joined together in a life that had never shown itself and was entirely new. In my second of understanding, I saw the past, the present and the future, merged in a humming universe.

I don't doubt either that I would never have returned to this planet if I'd lifted the shell once more and put the round hole to my eye. I can see now, of course, why every one of the treasure-seekers wanted to grasp hold of the future so much, trapped as they were in their vision of the past. Or was it the vanished piece of eight – Captain Flint's coin – they were really after? I'll never know.

At any rate, I'm glad enough to be in my room (with a headache, it's true) after falling to the ground on Treasure Island. I think often of Long John Silver who followed Captain Flint's directions and hopped ashore from the *Hispaniola* to go off and find the real treasure. And I admire his bravery. But his hell – his punishment – is precisely that he *did* find it. He has to stay on that barren atoll forever, gazing at the future of the universe.

My idea of hell would probably be to have to join him there. I'm sorry I didn't bring back the shell, of course, to show Dottie and my father and mother that I'd really been. (Of the sand in my clothes my mother simply said that I should not have gone out with a cold in the early morning to the garden.) My only hope is when I go to school, I suppose. 'Treasure Island,' I'll say, when the teacher opens up the atlas again. 'It's easy!' And I'll give the latitude and longitude, as Jim never did – '87° by 5°. But as near as nothing to the Equator, you know.'

It just seems sad that the one thing I'll never know is who survived the explosion of the submarine to sail round Cape Horn up the coast of South America, in search of a treasure more precious than any gold they had known. They were all – Squire Trelawney and Captain Smollett and Admiral Guinea and Arethusa and Dr Livesey – as bad as each other, as we now know.

But I wouldn't mind looking into the future one more time – to see them arrive at Coco Island and find Long John Silver there.

SUPER GRAN

Forrest Wilson

Super Gran Smith hurled herself at young Willard's football in a sliding tackle. 'Come on, laddie, give us a wee kick at your ball,' she cried. Willard stared, amazed. Only a minute ago she had been just a little old lady sitting on a park bench. But that was before the strange beam of blue light shot through her – the start of being Super Gran, with incredible speed, strength and X-ray eyes. But it was Edison who knew that Gran's miracle powers had come from a machine invented by her father, now stolen by the Inventor for his own plans to take over the world. Daunted by nothing, and gathering a force of Super Oldies, Super Gran goes forward to battle with the Inventor and his Super Toughies.

THE FOX BUSTERS

Dick King-Smith

The chickens of Foxearth Farm were a very special lot – they had long legs, they were quick witted, but most important of all, they could fly! They really could fly – up and away out of the reach of foxes.

The Foxearth Fowls found their names on bits of writing scattered about the Farm, like Fisons and Leyland, Trespassers and Beware Of. And one day Massey-Harris became the father of three chicks so exceptional that they were given brand-new names, for Ransome, Sims and Jefferies could fly faster, higher and further than any before them. And when a group of determined young foxes kept laying plans for one fiendishly cunning raid after another, the legendary three found a way of outwitting the most crafty of them. Not for nothing would they one day be known as the Fox Busters!

FLAMBARDS
THE EDGE OF THE CLOUD
FLAMBARDS IN SUMMER

K. M. Peyton

Twelve-year-old Christina is sent to live with her Uncle Russell and his two sons in their country house, Flambards. It's a strange unruly household that she grows up in during the years before the First World War: one she comes to love, hate and be inextricably bound up with. Later, she returns to Flambards as a young widow in search of comfort, and though haunted by painful memories, she is determined to forget the past and bring Flambards to life again. The Flambards trilogy was awarded both the 1969 Carnegie Medal and the 1970 Guardian Award for Children's Fiction.

THE GHOST'S COMPANION

ed. Peter Haining

Even if they have never seen a ghost themselves, most people know someone who claims to have seen one, so perhaps it's not so very surprising that Peter Haining has been able to collect together so many stories by authors who have themselves had supernatural experiences which have inspired their tales.

Rudyard Kipling's *My Own True Ghost Story*, about a haunted bungalow in India, is here; *Escort*, an eerie sea story about ships at war, is told by Daphne du Maurier, whose home by the sea in Cornwall made her so aware of the ghosts of generations of sailors lost at sea; *Aunt Jezebel's House* by Joan Aiken, about a most unusual small boy in a train . . . This is a thrilling selection for everyone who likes to sit safely by a warm fire and enjoy a good shudder.

WITCH'S BREW

ed. Alfred Hitchcock

A potent cauldron of the most grisly, heart-thumping witch stories ever recounted in the shuddering light of day! From E. F. Benson's tale of the vicar's daughter who is secretly inflamed with the taint of sorcery, to T. H. White's grievously wicked Madame Mim, or the witch who transforms her unwelcome visitors into nore manageable forms – frogs, maybe – there's not one of these sorceresses we'd cross broomsticks with!

THE BONGLEWEED

Helen Cresswell

Becky's father was head man at Pew Gardens and had always taken his work as seriously as a religion. To Becky it seemed rather silly to keep crossing one plant with another, so she wasn't particularly impressed when her father planted some unknown seeds in the tropical house on Monday and she found that by Wednesday they were two feet high. She christened them Bongleweed, thinking they were just a joke – until the ones she planted herself grew three feet in one night! And when it began clambering and creeping over the wall, people began to be frightened.

Heard about the Puffin Club?

. . . it's a way of finding out more about Puffin books and authors, of winning prizes (in competitions), sharing jokes, a secret code, and perhaps seeing your name in print! When you join you get a copy of our magazine, *Puffin Post*, sent to you four times a year, a badge and a membership book.

For details of subscription and an application form, send a stamped addressed envelope to:

The Puffin Club Dept A
Penguin Books Limited
Bath Road
Harmondsworth
Middlesex UB7 0DA

and if you live in Australia, please write to:

The Australian Puffin Club
Penguin Books Australia Limited
P.O. Box 257
Ringwood
Victoria 3134